[redacted] [redacted] [redacted]

STAR WARS

EPISODE III
REVENGE OF THE SITH

VOLUME TWO

ADAPTED FROM THE STORY
AND SCREENPLAY BY
GEORGE LUCAS

SCRIPT
MILES LANE

ART
DOUGLAS WHEATLEY

COLORS
CHRIS CHUCKRY

LETTERING
MICHAEL DAVID THOMAS

COVER ART
DAVE DORMAN

After being recalled to Coruscant from the Outer Rim Sieges, Obi-Wan Kenobi and Anakin Sky-walker effect a spectacular rescue—freeing Supreme Chancellor Palpatine from the clutches of Count Dooku and his cyborg henchman General Grievous. During the battle, Anakin kills Dooku, but Grievous escapes.

With Count Dooku dead, anticipation runs high that the Clone Wars will soon be ending. Only Chancellor Palpatine disagrees, saying the war will continue until General Grievous is destroyed.

The return to Coruscant culminates in a happy reunion between Anakin and the woman to whom he is secretly married—Padmé Amidala, the senator from Naboo. They have not seen each other in five months, and Padmé has important news: she is pregnant . . .

DARK HORSE COMICS

Spotlight

VISIT US AT
www.abdopublishing.com

Reinforced library bound edition published in 2010 by Spotlight, a division of the ABDO Group, 8000 West 78th Street, Edina, Minnesota 55439. Spotlight produces high-quality reinforced library bound editions for schools and libraries. Published by agreement with Dark Horse Comics, Inc., and Lucasfilm Ltd.

Library of Congress Cataloging-in-Publication Data

Lane, Miles.
  Star wars, episode III, revenge of the Sith / based on the story and screenplay by George Lucas ; Miles Lane, adaptation ; Doug Wheatley, art ; Chris Chuckry, colors ; Michael David Thomas, letters. -- Reinforced library bound ed.
     v. <1-4> cm.
  "Dark Horse."
  ISBN 978-1-59961-617-9 (volume 1) -- ISBN 978-1-59961-618-6 (volume 2) -- ISBN 978-1-59961-619-3 (volume 3) -- ISBN 978-1-59961-620-9 (volume 4)
  I. Lucas, George, 1944- II. Wheatley, Doug. III. Chuckry, Chris. IV. Thomas, Michael David. V. Dark Horse Comics. VI. Star Wars, episode III, revenge of the Sith (Motion picture) VII. Title. VIII. Title: Star wars, episode three, revenge of the Sith. IX. Title: Star wars, episode 3, revenge of the Sith. X. Title: Revenge of the Sith.
  PZ7.7.L36Std 2009
  741.5'973--dc22

                              2009002014

All Spotlight books have reinforced library bindings and
are manufactured in the United States of America.

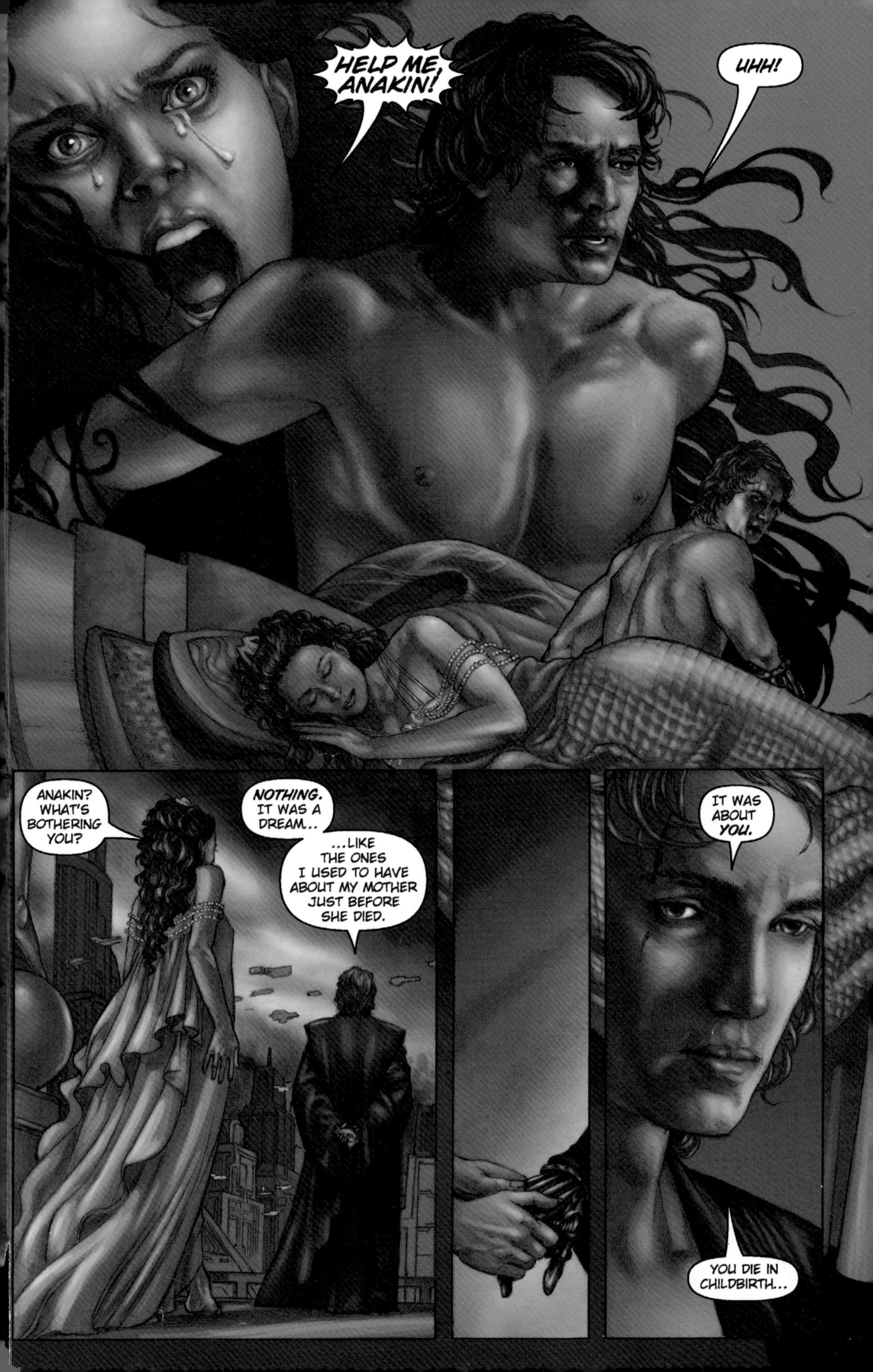
HELP ME, ANAKIN!
UHH!
ANAKIN? WHAT'S BOTHERING YOU?
NOTHING. IT WAS A DREAM...
...LIKE THE ONES I USED TO HAVE ABOUT MY MOTHER JUST BEFORE SHE DIED.
IT WAS ABOUT YOU.
YOU DIE IN CHILDBIRTH...

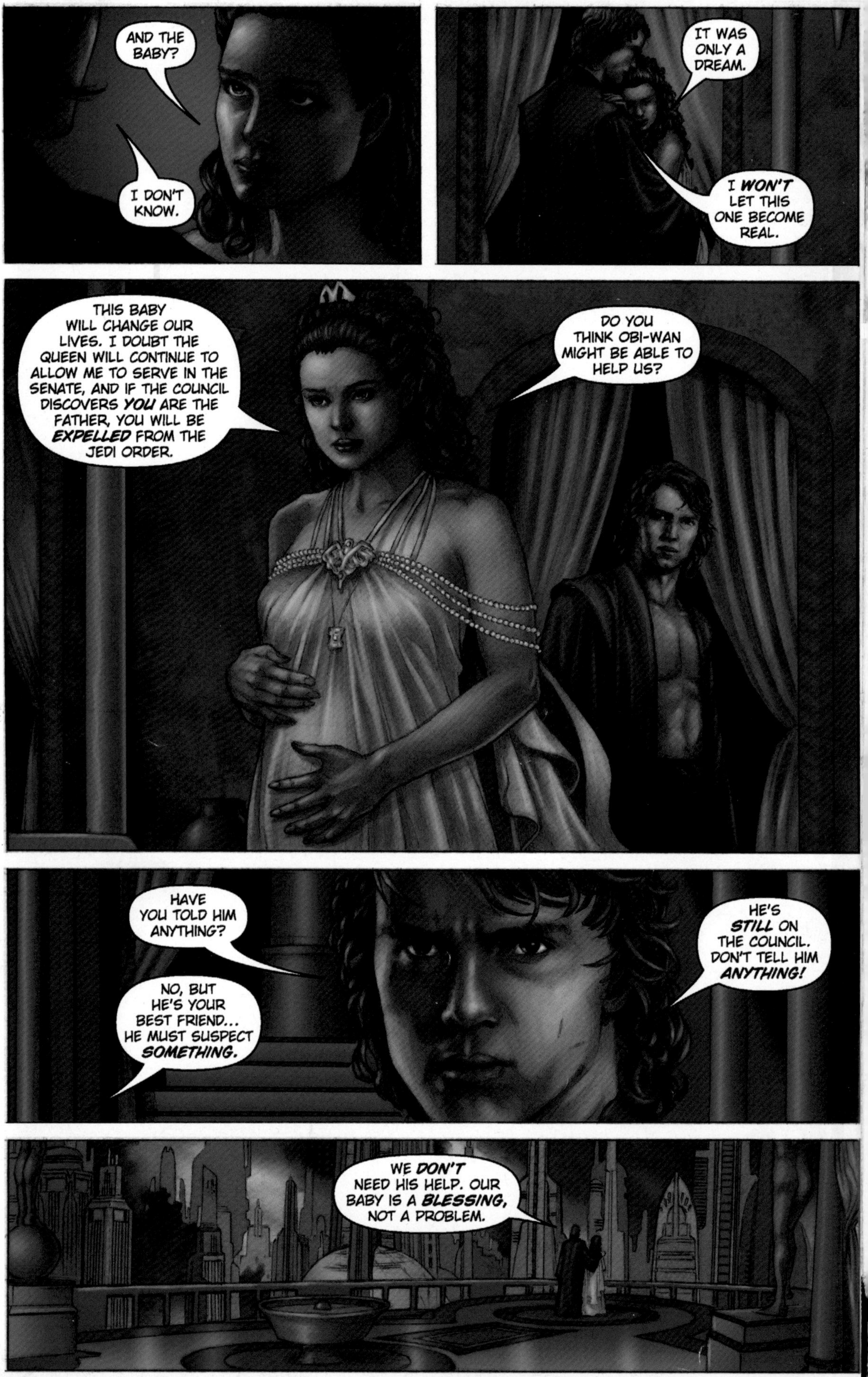
AND THE BABY?
I DON'T KNOW.
IT WAS ONLY A DREAM.
I WON'T LET THIS ONE BECOME REAL.
THIS BABY WILL CHANGE OUR LIVES. I DOUBT THE QUEEN WILL CONTINUE TO ALLOW ME TO SERVE IN THE SENATE, AND IF THE COUNCIL DISCOVERS YOU ARE THE FATHER, YOU WILL BE EXPELLED FROM THE JEDI ORDER.
DO YOU THINK OBI-WAN MIGHT BE ABLE TO HELP US?
HAVE YOU TOLD HIM ANYTHING?
NO, BUT HE'S YOUR BEST FRIEND... HE MUST SUSPECT SOMETHING.
HE'S STILL ON THE COUNCIL. DON'T TELL HIM ANYTHING!
WE DON'T NEED HIS HELP. OUR BABY IS A BLESSING, NOT A PROBLEM.

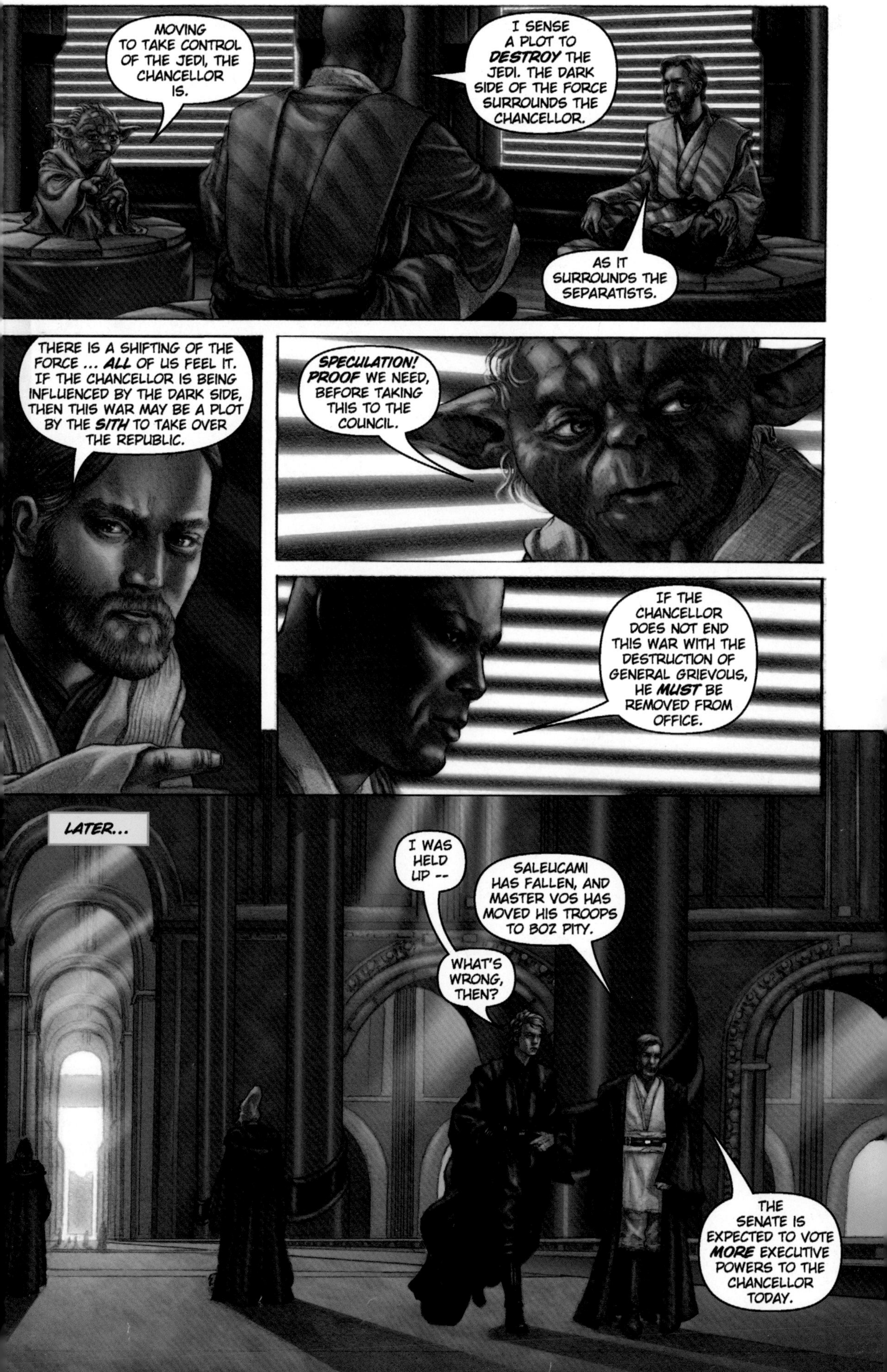
MOVING TO TAKE CONTROL OF THE JEDI, THE CHANCELLOR IS.
I SENSE A PLOT TO DESTROY THE JEDI. THE DARK SIDE OF THE FORCE SURROUNDS THE CHANCELLOR.
AS IT SURROUNDS THE SEPARATISTS.
THERE IS A SHIFTING OF THE FORCE ... ALL OF US FEEL IT. IF THE CHANCELLOR IS BEING INFLUENCED BY THE DARK SIDE, THEN THIS WAR MAY BE A PLOT BY THE SITH TO TAKE OVER THE REPUBLIC.
SPECULATION! PROOF WE NEED, BEFORE TAKING THIS TO THE COUNCIL.
IF THE CHANCELLOR DOES NOT END THIS WAR WITH THE DESTRUCTION OF GENERAL GRIEVOUS, HE MUST BE REMOVED FROM OFFICE.
LATER...
I WAS HELD UP --
SALEUCAMI HAS FALLEN, AND MASTER VOS HAS MOVED HIS TROOPS TO BOZ PITY.
WHAT'S WRONG, THEN?
THE SENATE IS EXPECTED TO VOTE MORE EXECUTIVE POWERS TO THE CHANCELLOR TODAY.

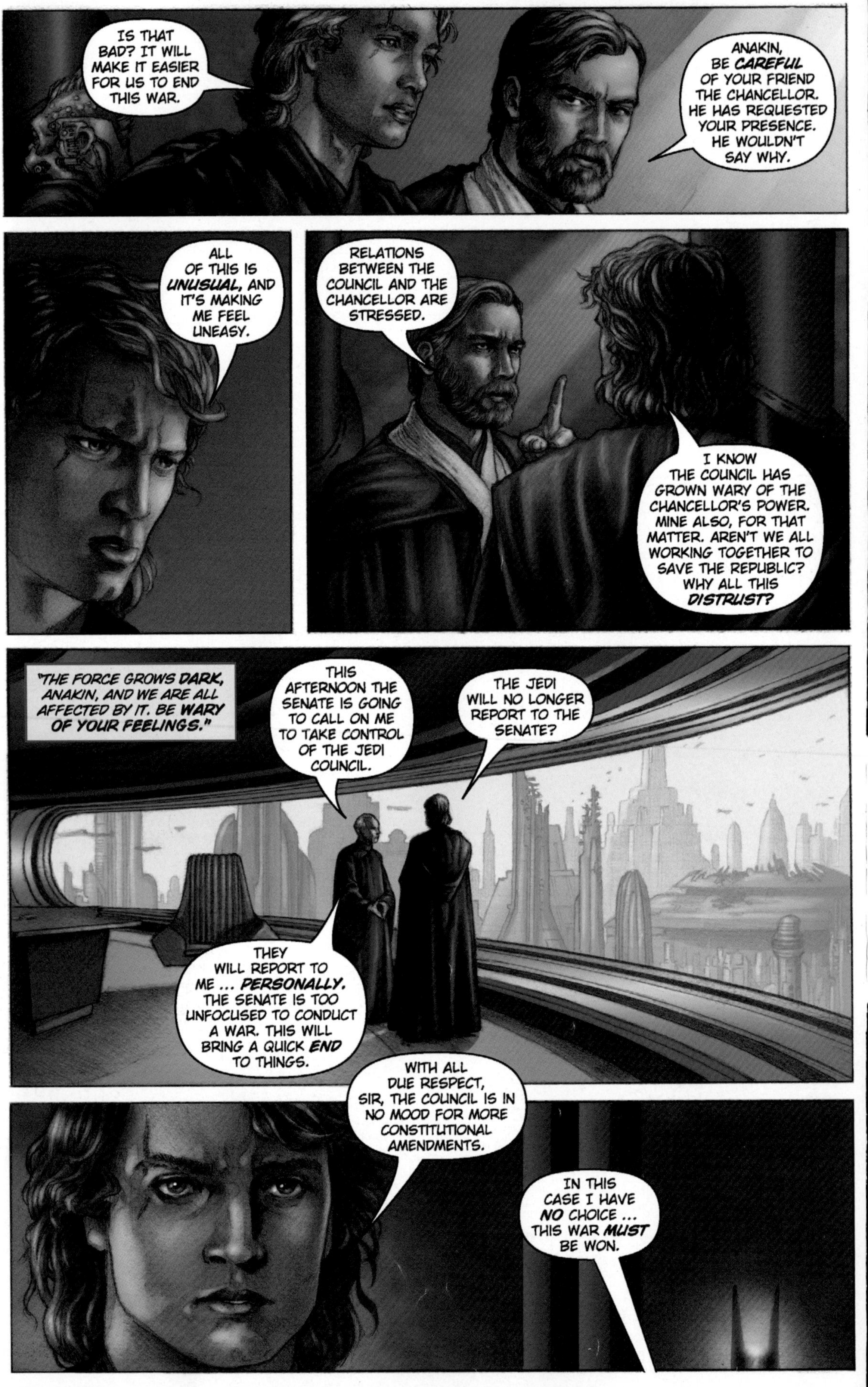
IS THAT BAD? IT WILL MAKE IT EASIER FOR US TO END THIS WAR.
ANAKIN, BE CAREFUL OF YOUR FRIEND THE CHANCELLOR. HE HAS REQUESTED YOUR PRESENCE. HE WOULDN'T SAY WHY.
ALL OF THIS IS UNUSUAL, AND IT'S MAKING ME FEEL UNEASY.
RELATIONS BETWEEN THE COUNCIL AND THE CHANCELLOR ARE STRESSED.
I KNOW THE COUNCIL HAS GROWN WARY OF THE CHANCELLOR'S POWER. MINE ALSO, FOR THAT MATTER. AREN'T WE ALL WORKING TOGETHER TO SAVE THE REPUBLIC? WHY ALL THIS DISTRUST?
"THE FORCE GROWS DARK, ANAKIN, AND WE ARE ALL AFFECTED BY IT. BE WARY OF YOUR FEELINGS."
THIS AFTERNOON THE SENATE IS GOING TO CALL ON ME TO TAKE CONTROL OF THE JEDI COUNCIL.
THE JEDI WILL NO LONGER REPORT TO THE SENATE?
THEY WILL REPORT TO ME ... PERSONALLY. THE SENATE IS TOO UNFOCUSED TO CONDUCT A WAR. THIS WILL BRING A QUICK END TO THINGS.
WITH ALL DUE RESPECT, SIR, THE COUNCIL IS IN NO MOOD FOR MORE CONSTITUTIONAL AMENDMENTS.
IN THIS CASE I HAVE NO CHOICE ... THIS WAR MUST BE WON.

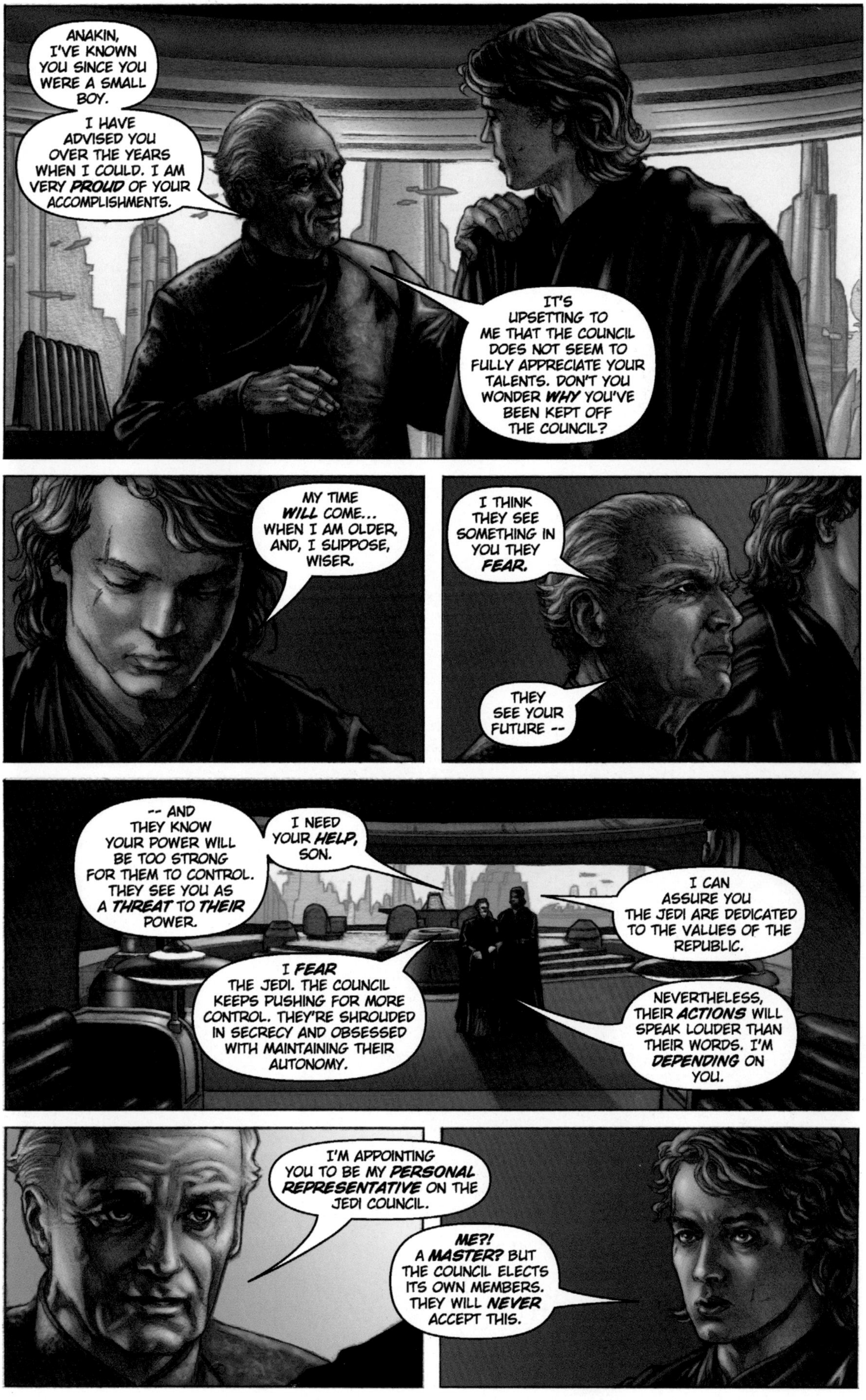
ANAKIN, I'VE KNOWN YOU SINCE YOU WERE A SMALL BOY.
I HAVE ADVISED YOU OVER THE YEARS WHEN I COULD. I AM VERY PROUD OF YOUR ACCOMPLISHMENTS.
IT'S UPSETTING TO ME THAT THE COUNCIL DOES NOT SEEM TO FULLY APPRECIATE YOUR TALENTS. DON'T YOU WONDER WHY YOU'VE BEEN KEPT OFF THE COUNCIL?
MY TIME WILL COME... WHEN I AM OLDER, AND, I SUPPOSE, WISER.
I THINK THEY SEE SOMETHING IN YOU THEY FEAR.
THEY SEE YOUR FUTURE --
-- AND THEY KNOW YOUR POWER WILL BE TOO STRONG FOR THEM TO CONTROL. THEY SEE YOU AS A THREAT TO THEIR POWER.
I NEED YOUR HELP, SON.
I CAN ASSURE YOU THE JEDI ARE DEDICATED TO THE VALUES OF THE REPUBLIC.
I FEAR THE JEDI. THE COUNCIL KEEPS PUSHING FOR MORE CONTROL. THEY'RE SHROUDED IN SECRECY AND OBSESSED WITH MAINTAINING THEIR AUTONOMY.
NEVERTHELESS, THEIR ACTIONS WILL SPEAK LOUDER THAN THEIR WORDS. I'M DEPENDING ON YOU.
I'M APPOINTING YOU TO BE MY PERSONAL REPRESENTATIVE ON THE JEDI COUNCIL.
ME?! A MASTER? BUT THE COUNCIL ELECTS ITS OWN MEMBERS. THEY WILL NEVER ACCEPT THIS.

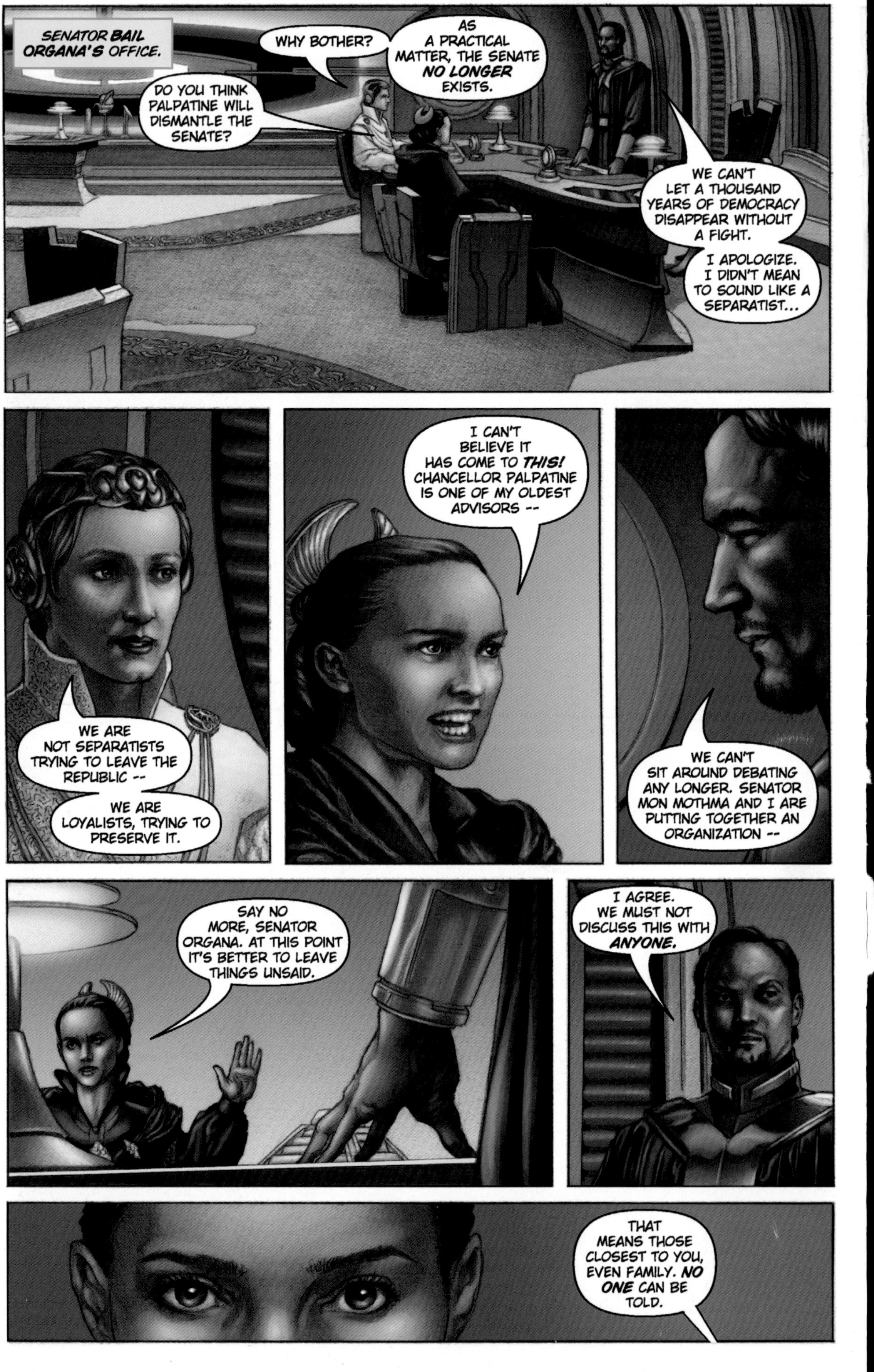
SENATOR BAIL ORGANA'S OFFICE.
DO YOU THINK PALPATINE WILL DISMANTLE THE SENATE?
WHY BOTHER?
AS A PRACTICAL MATTER, THE SENATE NO LONGER EXISTS.
WE CAN'T LET A THOUSAND YEARS OF DEMOCRACY DISAPPEAR WITHOUT A FIGHT.
I APOLOGIZE. I DIDN'T MEAN TO SOUND LIKE A SEPARATIST...
WE ARE NOT SEPARATISTS TRYING TO LEAVE THE REPUBLIC --
WE ARE LOYALISTS, TRYING TO PRESERVE IT.
I CAN'T BELIEVE IT HAS COME TO THIS! CHANCELLOR PALPATINE IS ONE OF MY OLDEST ADVISORS --
WE CAN'T SIT AROUND DEBATING ANY LONGER. SENATOR MON MOTHMA AND I ARE PUTTING TOGETHER AN ORGANIZATION --
SAY NO MORE, SENATOR ORGANA. AT THIS POINT IT'S BETTER TO LEAVE THINGS UNSAID.
I AGREE. WE MUST NOT DISCUSS THIS WITH ANYONE.
THAT MEANS THOSE CLOSEST TO YOU, EVEN FAMILY. NO ONE CAN BE TOLD.

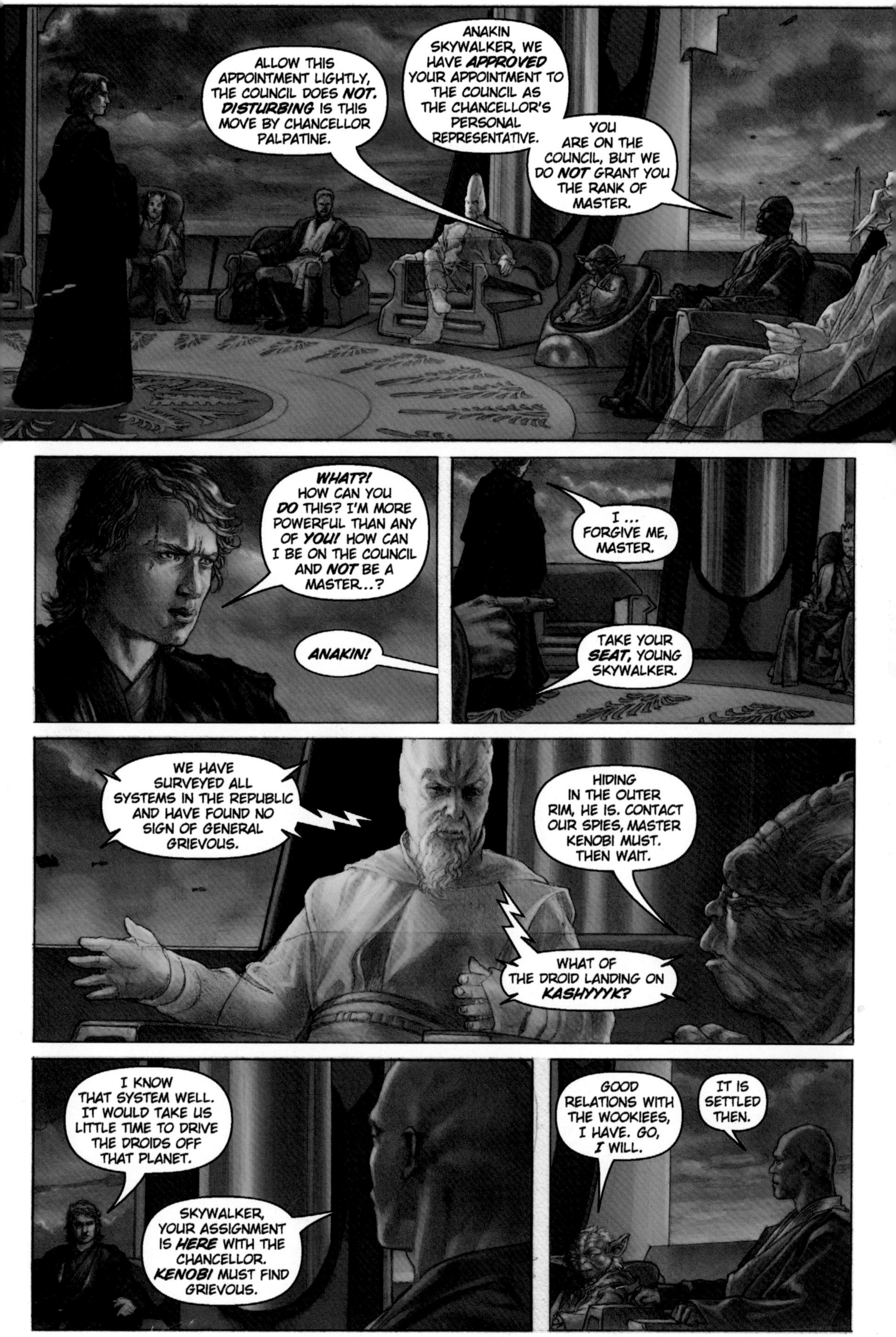

ALLOW THIS APPOINTMENT LIGHTLY, THE COUNCIL DOES *NOT.* *DISTURBING* IS THIS MOVE BY CHANCELLOR PALPATINE.
ANAKIN SKYWALKER, WE HAVE *APPROVED* YOUR APPOINTMENT TO THE COUNCIL AS THE CHANCELLOR'S PERSONAL REPRESENTATIVE.
YOU ARE ON THE COUNCIL, BUT WE DO *NOT* GRANT YOU THE RANK OF MASTER.
WHAT?! HOW CAN YOU *DO* THIS? I'M MORE POWERFUL THAN ANY OF *YOU!* HOW CAN I BE ON THE COUNCIL AND *NOT* BE A MASTER...?
ANAKIN!
I... FORGIVE ME, MASTER.
TAKE YOUR *SEAT,* YOUNG SKYWALKER.
WE HAVE SURVEYED ALL SYSTEMS IN THE REPUBLIC AND HAVE FOUND NO SIGN OF GENERAL GRIEVOUS.
HIDING IN THE OUTER RIM, HE IS. CONTACT OUR SPIES, MASTER KENOBI MUST. THEN WAIT.
WHAT OF THE DROID LANDING ON *KASHYYYK?*
I KNOW THAT SYSTEM WELL. IT WOULD TAKE US LITTLE TIME TO DRIVE THE DROIDS OFF THAT PLANET.
SKYWALKER, YOUR ASSIGNMENT IS *HERE* WITH THE CHANCELLOR. *KENOBI* MUST FIND GRIEVOUS.
GOOD RELATIONS WITH THE WOOKIEES, I HAVE. GO, *I* WILL.
IT IS SETTLED THEN.

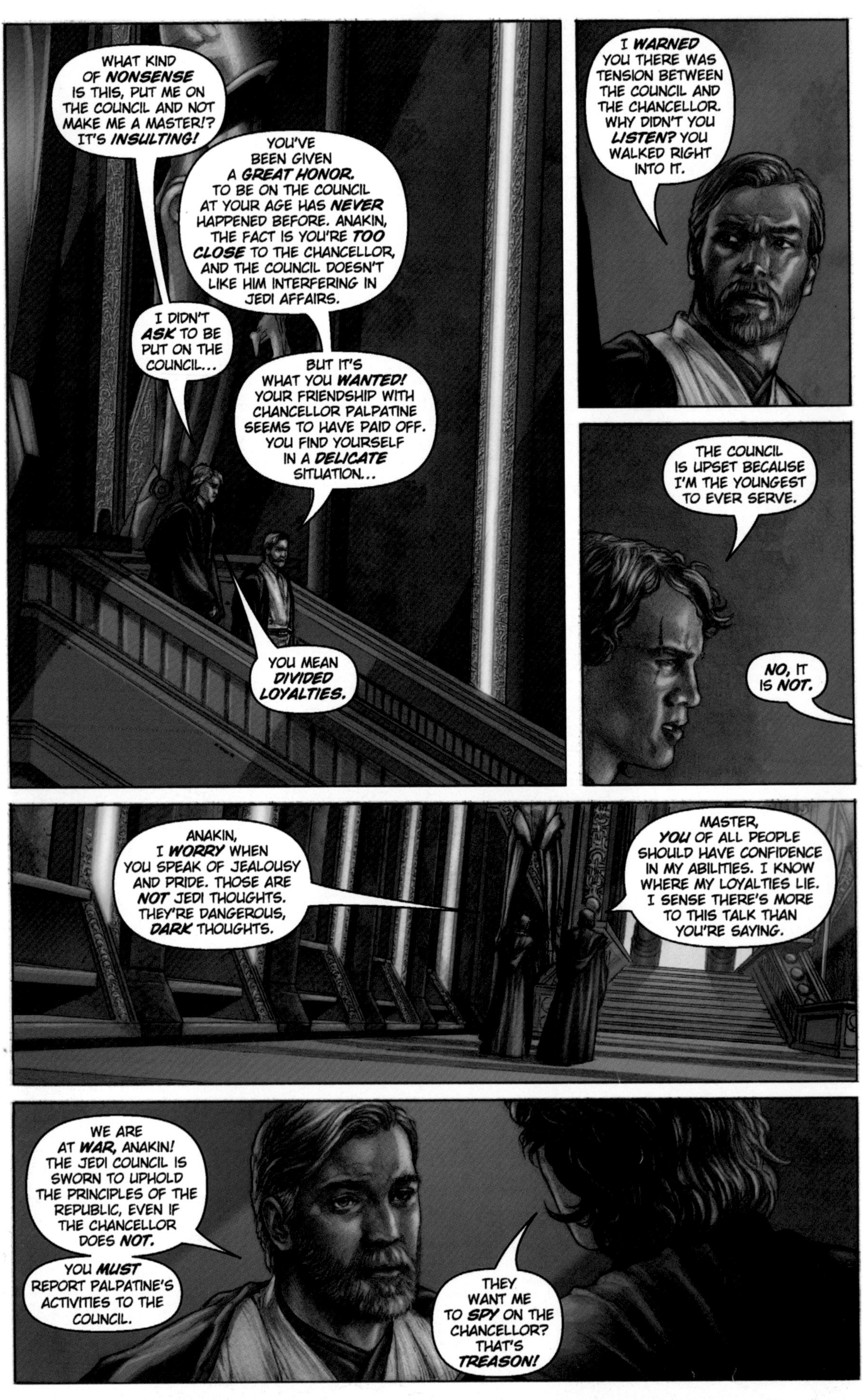
WHAT KIND OF NONSENSE IS THIS, PUT ME ON THE COUNCIL AND NOT MAKE ME A MASTER!? IT'S INSULTING!
YOU'VE BEEN GIVEN A GREAT HONOR. TO BE ON THE COUNCIL AT YOUR AGE HAS NEVER HAPPENED BEFORE. ANAKIN, THE FACT IS YOU'RE TOO CLOSE TO THE CHANCELLOR, AND THE COUNCIL DOESN'T LIKE HIM INTERFERING IN JEDI AFFAIRS.
I DIDN'T ASK TO BE PUT ON THE COUNCIL...
BUT IT'S WHAT YOU WANTED! YOUR FRIENDSHIP WITH CHANCELLOR PALPATINE SEEMS TO HAVE PAID OFF. YOU FIND YOURSELF IN A DELICATE SITUATION...
YOU MEAN DIVIDED LOYALTIES.
I WARNED YOU THERE WAS TENSION BETWEEN THE COUNCIL AND THE CHANCELLOR. WHY DIDN'T YOU LISTEN? YOU WALKED RIGHT INTO IT.
THE COUNCIL IS UPSET BECAUSE I'M THE YOUNGEST TO EVER SERVE.
NO, IT IS NOT.
ANAKIN, I WORRY WHEN YOU SPEAK OF JEALOUSY AND PRIDE. THOSE ARE NOT JEDI THOUGHTS. THEY'RE DANGEROUS, DARK THOUGHTS.
MASTER, YOU OF ALL PEOPLE SHOULD HAVE CONFIDENCE IN MY ABILITIES. I KNOW WHERE MY LOYALTIES LIE. I SENSE THERE'S MORE TO THIS TALK THAN YOU'RE SAYING.
WE ARE AT WAR, ANAKIN! THE JEDI COUNCIL IS SWORN TO UPHOLD THE PRINCIPLES OF THE REPUBLIC, EVEN IF THE CHANCELLOR DOES NOT.
YOU MUST REPORT PALPATINE'S ACTIVITIES TO THE COUNCIL.
THEY WANT ME TO SPY ON THE CHANCELLOR? THAT'S TREASON!

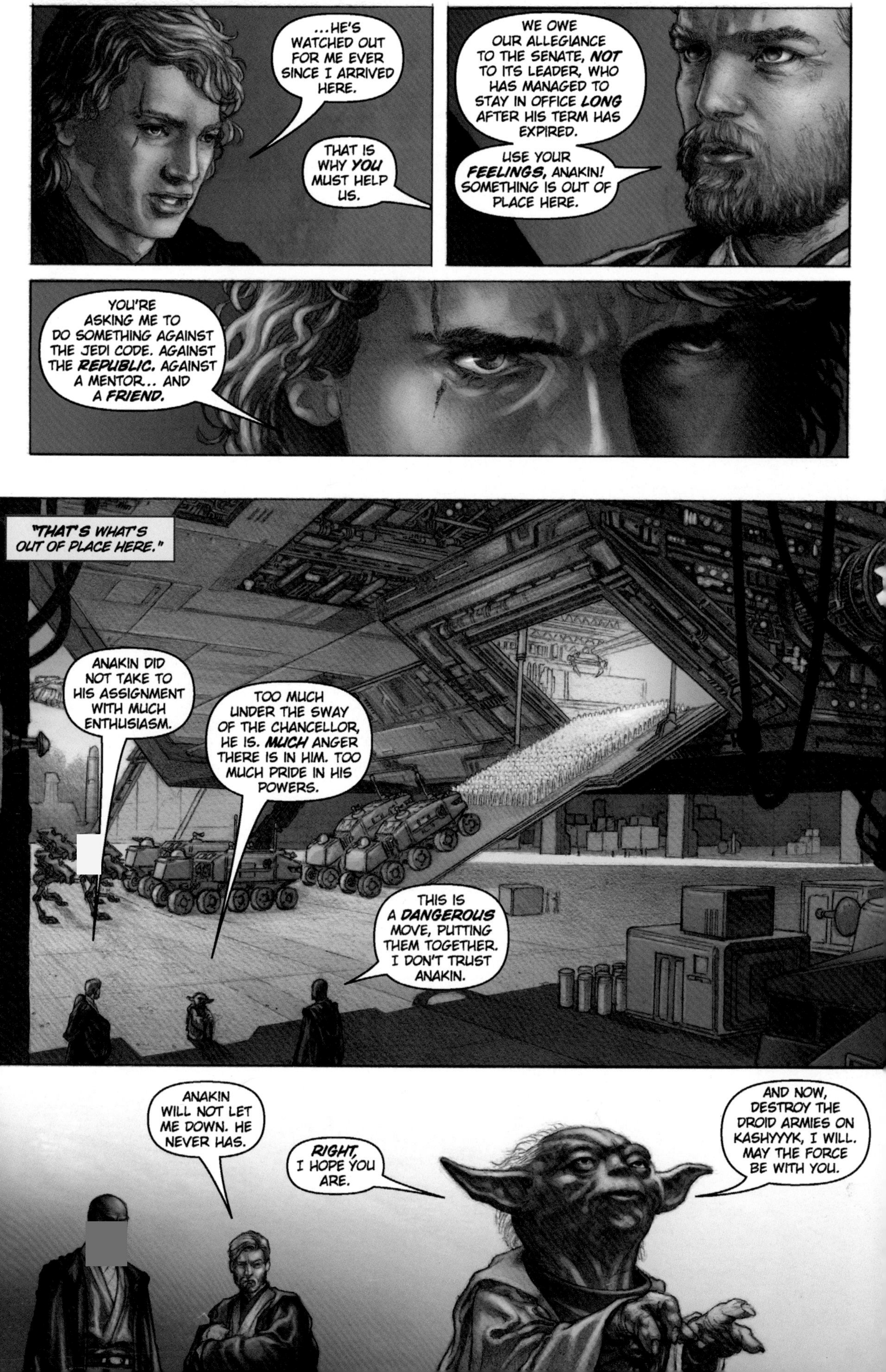
...HE'S WATCHED OUT FOR ME EVER SINCE I ARRIVED HERE.
THAT IS WHY *YOU* MUST HELP US.
WE OWE OUR ALLEGIANCE TO THE SENATE, *NOT* TO ITS LEADER, WHO HAS MANAGED TO STAY IN OFFICE *LONG* AFTER HIS TERM HAS EXPIRED.
USE YOUR *FEELINGS,* ANAKIN! SOMETHING IS OUT OF PLACE HERE.
YOU'RE ASKING ME TO DO SOMETHING AGAINST THE JEDI CODE. AGAINST THE *REPUBLIC.* AGAINST A MENTOR... AND A *FRIEND.*
"THAT'S WHAT'S OUT OF PLACE HERE."
ANAKIN DID NOT TAKE TO HIS ASSIGNMENT WITH MUCH ENTHUSIASM.
TOO MUCH UNDER THE SWAY OF THE CHANCELLOR, HE IS. *MUCH* ANGER THERE IS IN HIM. TOO MUCH PRIDE IN HIS POWERS.
THIS IS A *DANGEROUS* MOVE, PUTTING THEM TOGETHER. I DON'T TRUST ANAKIN.
ANAKIN WILL NOT LET ME DOWN. HE NEVER HAS.
RIGHT, I HOPE YOU ARE.
AND NOW, DESTROY THE DROID ARMIES ON KASHYYYK, I WILL. MAY THE FORCE BE WITH YOU.

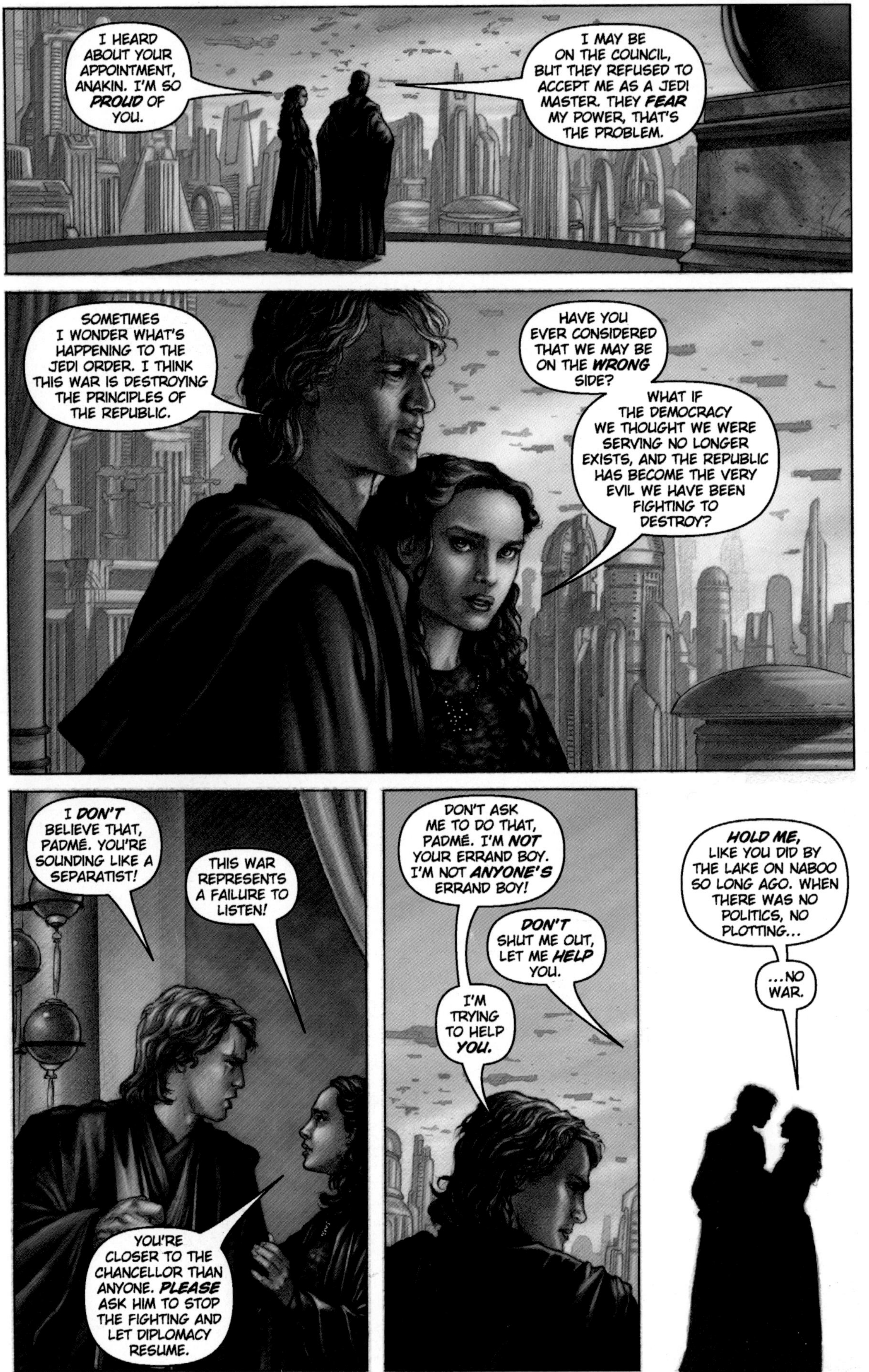
I HEARD ABOUT YOUR APPOINTMENT, ANAKIN. I'M SO PROUD OF YOU.
I MAY BE ON THE COUNCIL, BUT THEY REFUSED TO ACCEPT ME AS A JEDI MASTER. THEY FEAR MY POWER, THAT'S THE PROBLEM.
SOMETIMES I WONDER WHAT'S HAPPENING TO THE JEDI ORDER. I THINK THIS WAR IS DESTROYING THE PRINCIPLES OF THE REPUBLIC.
HAVE YOU EVER CONSIDERED THAT WE MAY BE ON THE WRONG SIDE?
WHAT IF THE DEMOCRACY WE THOUGHT WE WERE SERVING NO LONGER EXISTS, AND THE REPUBLIC HAS BECOME THE VERY EVIL WE HAVE BEEN FIGHTING TO DESTROY?
I DON'T BELIEVE THAT, PADMÉ. YOU'RE SOUNDING LIKE A SEPARATIST!
THIS WAR REPRESENTS A FAILURE TO LISTEN!
YOU'RE CLOSER TO THE CHANCELLOR THAN ANYONE. PLEASE ASK HIM TO STOP THE FIGHTING AND LET DIPLOMACY RESUME.
DON'T ASK ME TO DO THAT, PADMÉ. I'M NOT YOUR ERRAND BOY. I'M NOT ANYONE'S ERRAND BOY!
DON'T SHUT ME OUT, LET ME HELP YOU.
I'M TRYING TO HELP YOU.
HOLD ME, LIKE YOU DID BY THE LAKE ON NABOO SO LONG AGO. WHEN THERE WAS NO POLITICS, NO PLOTTING...
...NO WAR.

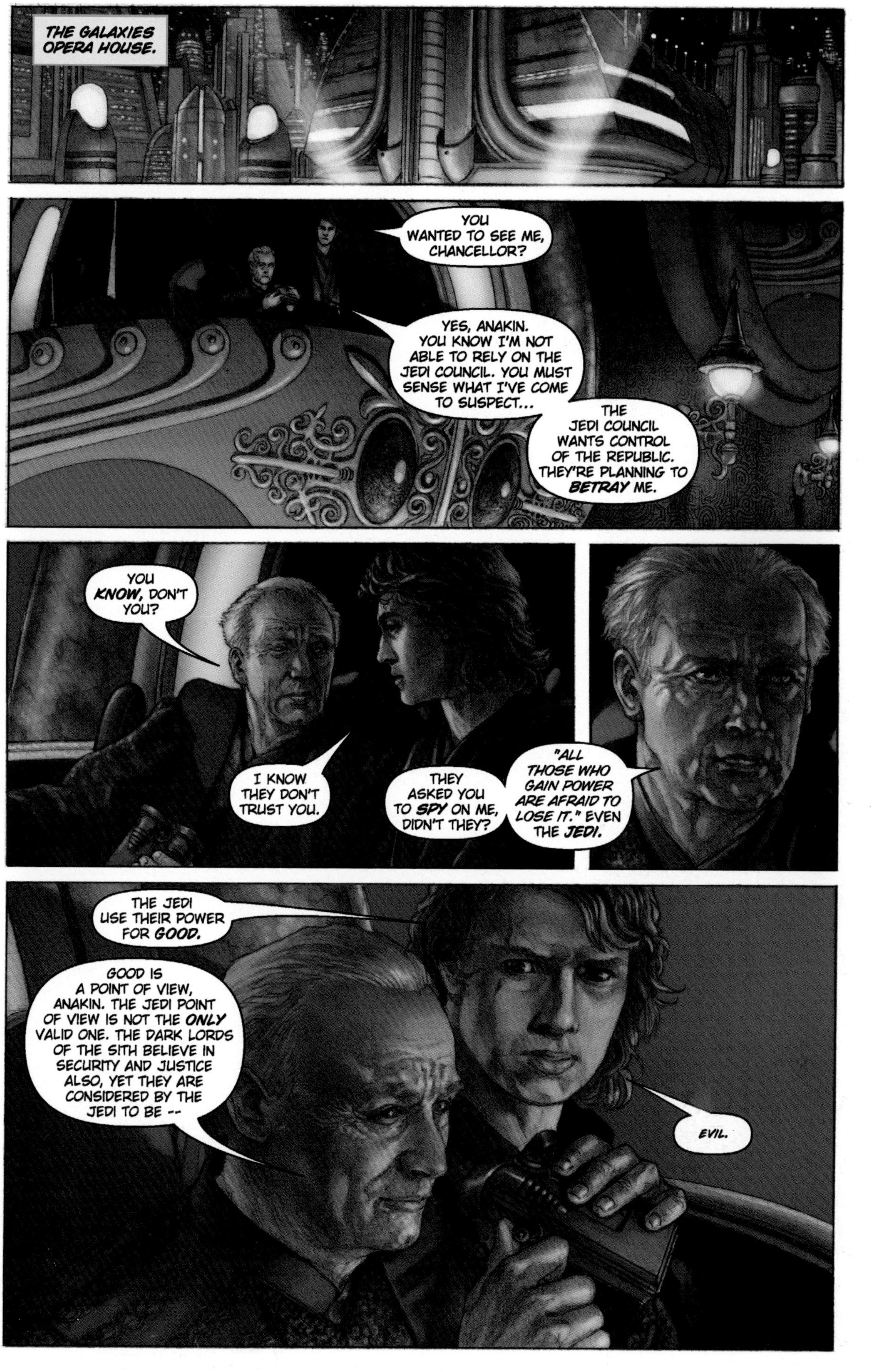
THE GALAXIES OPERA HOUSE.
YOU WANTED TO SEE ME, CHANCELLOR?
YES, ANAKIN. YOU KNOW I'M NOT ABLE TO RELY ON THE JEDI COUNCIL. YOU MUST SENSE WHAT I'VE COME TO SUSPECT...
THE JEDI COUNCIL WANTS CONTROL OF THE REPUBLIC. THEY'RE PLANNING TO BETRAY ME.
YOU KNOW, DON'T YOU?
I KNOW THEY DON'T TRUST YOU.
THEY ASKED YOU TO SPY ON ME, DIDN'T THEY?
"ALL THOSE WHO GAIN POWER ARE AFRAID TO LOSE IT." EVEN THE JEDI.
THE JEDI USE THEIR POWER FOR GOOD.
GOOD IS A POINT OF VIEW, ANAKIN. THE JEDI POINT OF VIEW IS NOT THE ONLY VALID ONE. THE DARK LORDS OF THE SITH BELIEVE IN SECURITY AND JUSTICE ALSO, YET THEY ARE CONSIDERED BY THE JEDI TO BE --
EVIL.

YET THE SITH AND THE JEDI ARE SIMILAR IN ALMOST EVERY WAY -- *INCLUDING* THEIR QUEST FOR GREATER POWER. THE *DIFFERENCE* BETWEEN THE TWO IS THAT THE SITH ARE *NOT AFRAID* OF THE DARK SIDE OF THE FORCE.

THAT IS WHY *THEY* ARE MORE POWERFUL.

THE SITH RELY ON THEIR PASSION FOR THEIR STRENGTH. THEY THINK *INWARD*, ONLY ABOUT THEMSELVES. THE JEDI ARE *SELFLESS* ... THEY ONLY CARE ABOUT *OTHERS*.

THE FEAR OF *LOSING* POWER IS A WEAKNESS OF *BOTH* THE JEDI AND THE SITH.

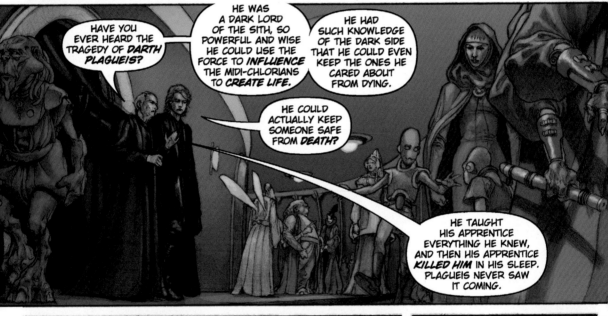

HAVE YOU EVER HEARD THE TRAGEDY OF *DARTH PLAGUEIS*?

HE WAS A DARK LORD OF THE SITH, SO POWERFUL AND WISE HE COULD USE THE FORCE TO *INFLUENCE* THE MIDI-CHLORIANS TO *CREATE LIFE.*

HE HAD SUCH KNOWLEDGE OF THE DARK SIDE THAT HE COULD EVEN KEEP THE ONES HE CARED ABOUT FROM DYING.

HE COULD ACTUALLY KEEP SOMEONE SAFE FROM *DEATH*?

HE TAUGHT HIS APPRENTICE EVERYTHING HE KNEW, AND THEN HIS APPRENTICE *KILLED HIM* IN HIS SLEEP. PLAGUEIS NEVER SAW IT COMING.

HE COULD SAVE *OTHERS* FROM DEATH, BUT NOT *HIMSELF.*

IS IT POSSIBLE TO *LEARN* THIS POWER?

NOT FROM A JEDI.

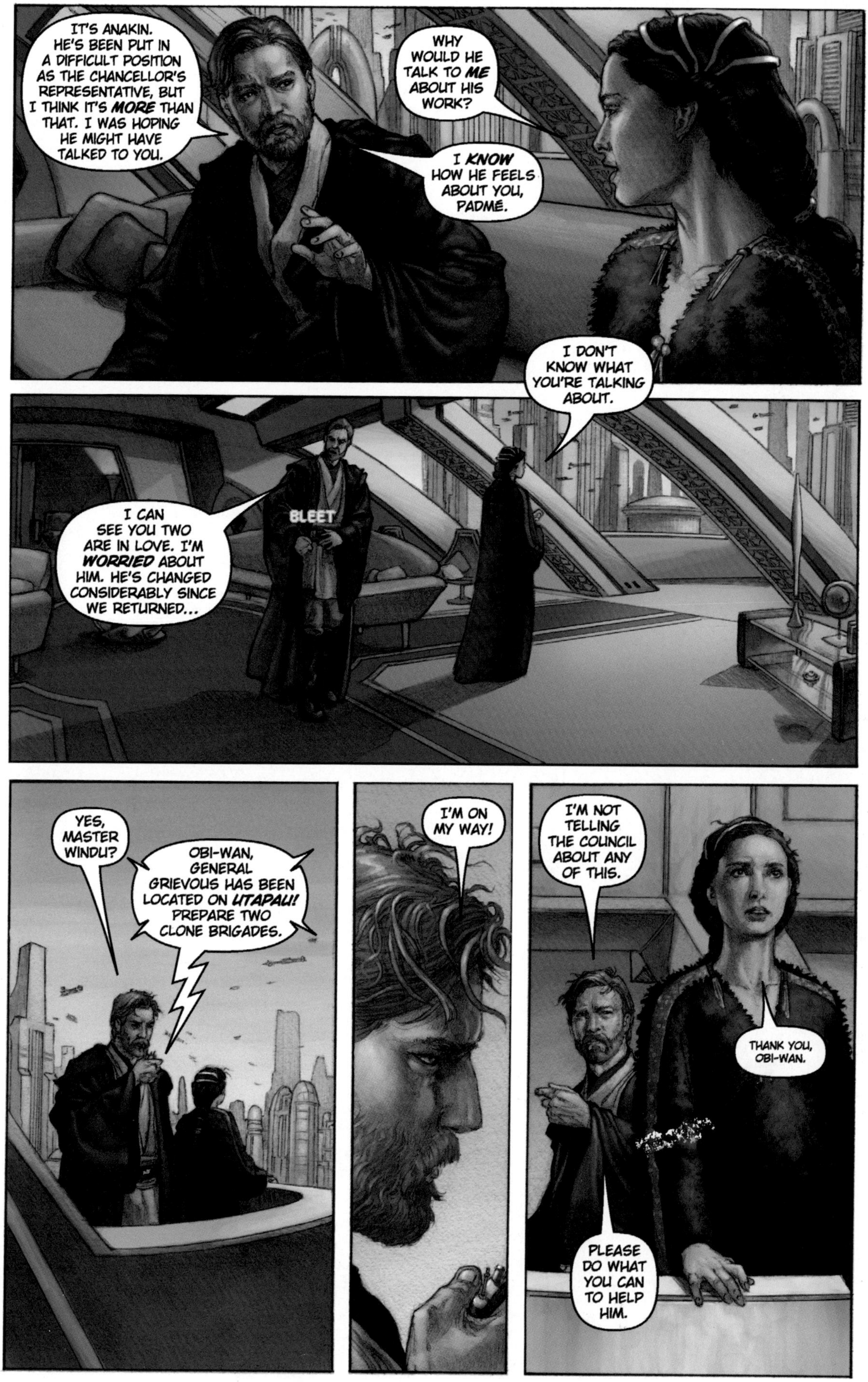
IT'S ANAKIN. HE'S BEEN PUT IN A DIFFICULT POSITION AS THE CHANCELLOR'S REPRESENTATIVE, BUT I THINK IT'S MORE THAN THAT. I WAS HOPING HE MIGHT HAVE TALKED TO YOU.
WHY WOULD HE TALK TO ME ABOUT HIS WORK?
I KNOW HOW HE FEELS ABOUT YOU, PADMÉ.
I DON'T KNOW WHAT YOU'RE TALKING ABOUT.
I CAN SEE YOU TWO ARE IN LOVE. I'M WORRIED ABOUT HIM. HE'S CHANGED CONSIDERABLY SINCE WE RETURNED...
BLEET
YES, MASTER WINDU?
OBI-WAN, GENERAL GRIEVOUS HAS BEEN LOCATED ON UTAPAU! PREPARE TWO CLONE BRIGADES.
I'M ON MY WAY!
I'M NOT TELLING THE COUNCIL ABOUT ANY OF THIS.
THANK YOU, OBI-WAN.
PLEASE DO WHAT YOU CAN TO HELP HIM.

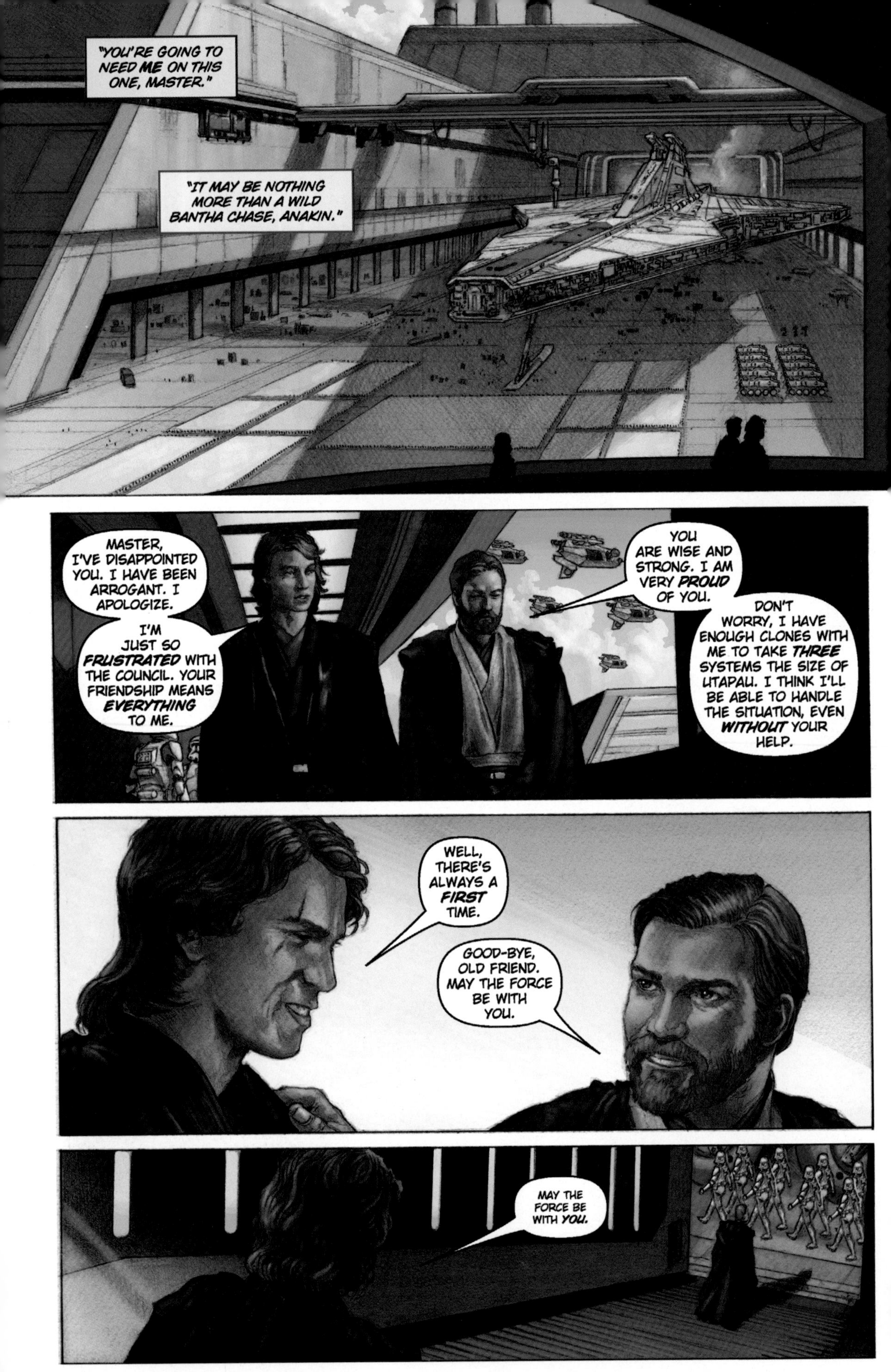
"YOU'RE GOING TO NEED **ME** ON THIS ONE, MASTER."
"IT MAY BE NOTHING MORE THAN A WILD BANTHA CHASE, ANAKIN."
MASTER, I'VE DISAPPOINTED YOU. I HAVE BEEN ARROGANT. I APOLOGIZE.
I'M JUST SO **FRUSTRATED** WITH THE COUNCIL. YOUR FRIENDSHIP MEANS **EVERYTHING** TO ME.
YOU ARE WISE AND STRONG. I AM VERY **PROUD** OF YOU.
DON'T WORRY, I HAVE ENOUGH CLONES WITH ME TO TAKE **THREE** SYSTEMS THE SIZE OF UTAPAU. I THINK I'LL BE ABLE TO HANDLE THE SITUATION, EVEN **WITHOUT** YOUR HELP.
WELL, THERE'S ALWAYS A **FIRST** TIME.
GOOD-BYE, OLD FRIEND. MAY THE FORCE BE WITH YOU.
MAY THE FORCE BE WITH **YOU.**

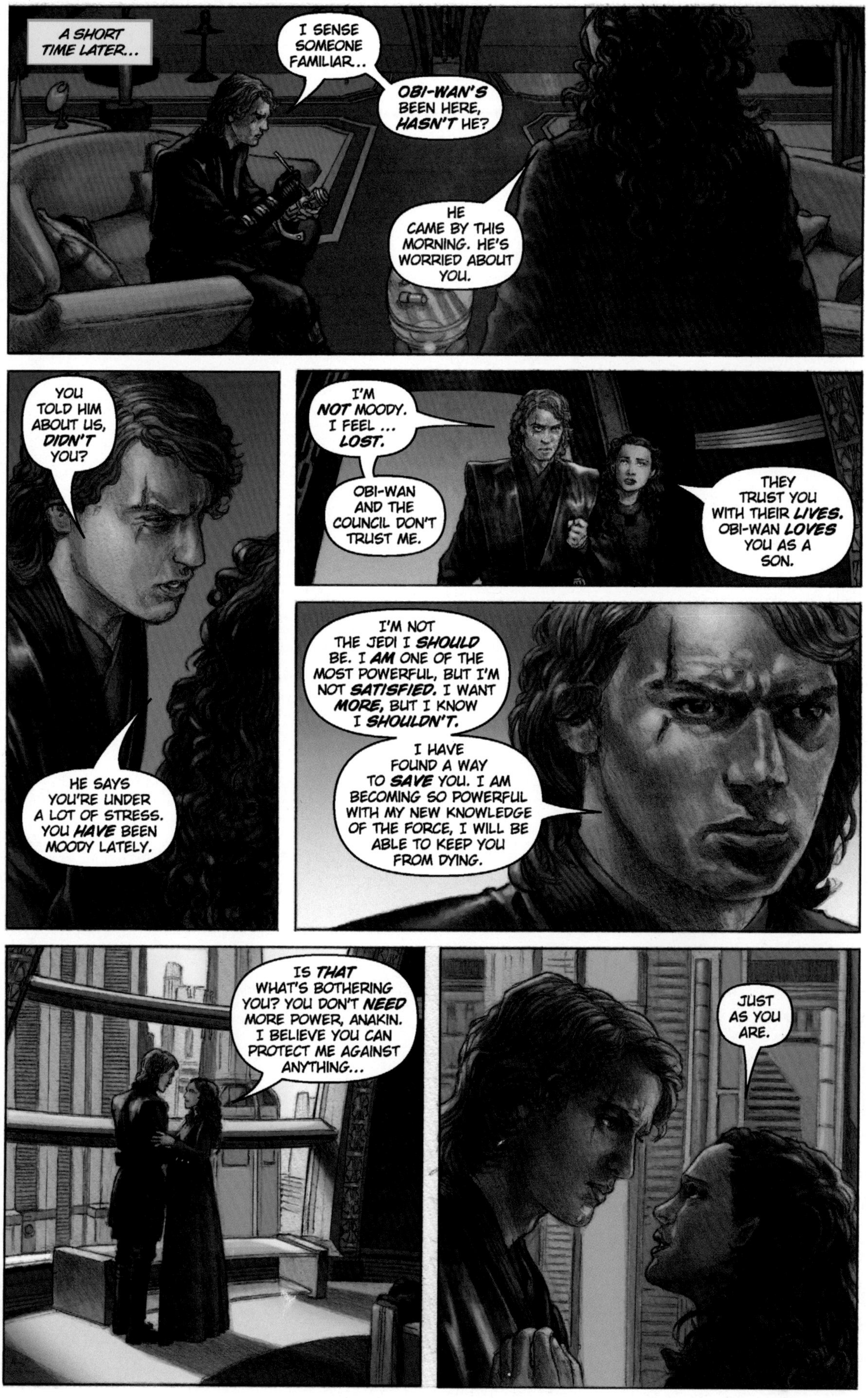

A SHORT TIME LATER...
I SENSE SOMEONE FAMILIAR...
OBI-WAN'S BEEN HERE, HASN'T HE?
HE CAME BY THIS MORNING. HE'S WORRIED ABOUT YOU.
YOU TOLD HIM ABOUT US, DIDN'T YOU?
HE SAYS YOU'RE UNDER A LOT OF STRESS. YOU HAVE BEEN MOODY LATELY.
I'M NOT MOODY. I FEEL ... LOST.
OBI-WAN AND THE COUNCIL DON'T TRUST ME.
THEY TRUST YOU WITH THEIR LIVES. OBI-WAN LOVES YOU AS A SON.
I'M NOT THE JEDI I SHOULD BE. I AM ONE OF THE MOST POWERFUL, BUT I'M NOT SATISFIED. I WANT MORE, BUT I KNOW I SHOULDN'T.
I HAVE FOUND A WAY TO SAVE YOU. I AM BECOMING SO POWERFUL WITH MY NEW KNOWLEDGE OF THE FORCE, I WILL BE ABLE TO KEEP YOU FROM DYING.
IS THAT WHAT'S BOTHERING YOU? YOU DON'T NEED MORE POWER, ANAKIN. I BELIEVE YOU CAN PROTECT ME AGAINST ANYTHING...
JUST AS YOU ARE.

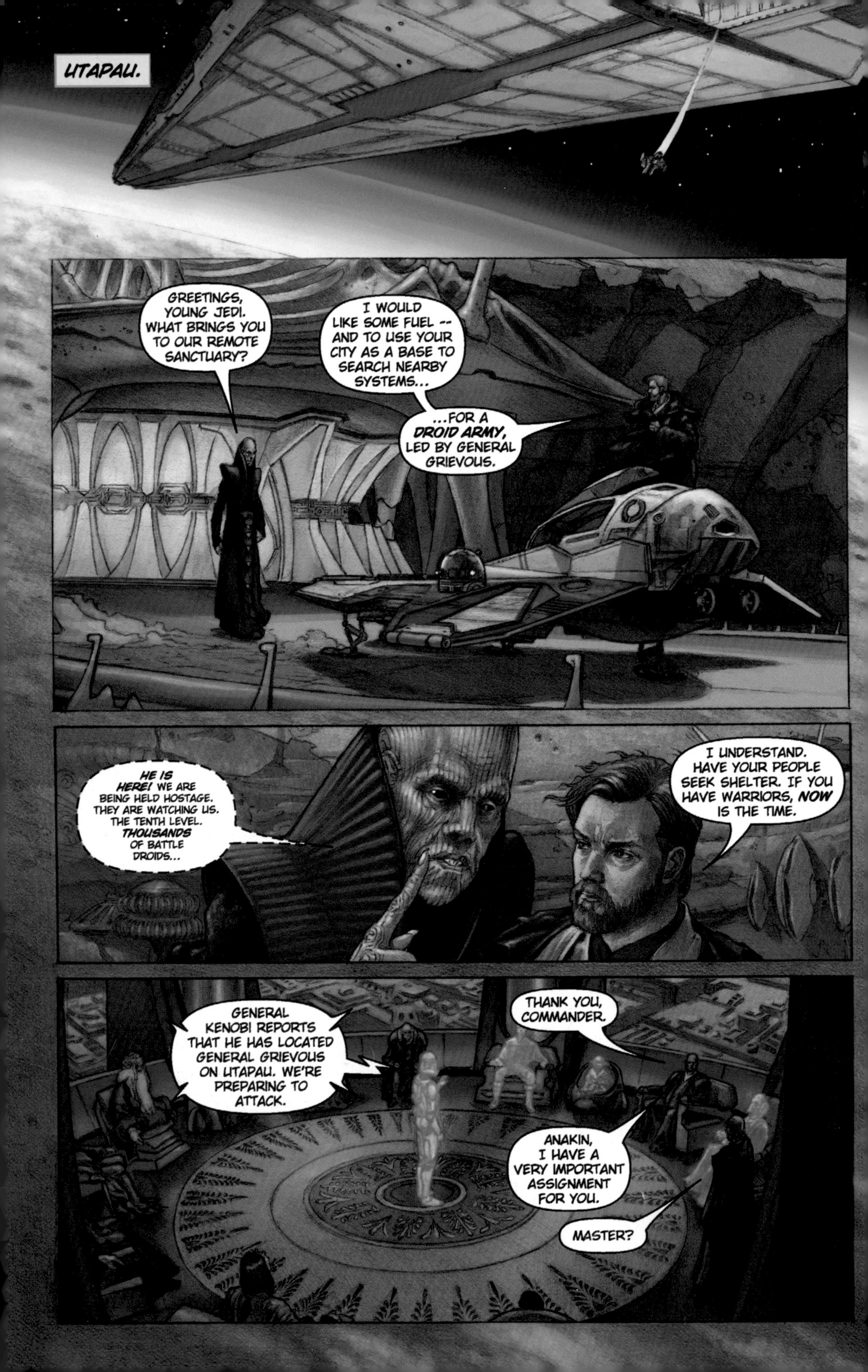
UTAPAU.
GREETINGS, YOUNG JEDI. WHAT BRINGS YOU TO OUR REMOTE SANCTUARY?
I WOULD LIKE SOME FUEL -- AND TO USE YOUR CITY AS A BASE TO SEARCH NEARBY SYSTEMS...
...FOR A DROID ARMY, LED BY GENERAL GRIEVOUS.
HE IS HERE! WE ARE BEING HELD HOSTAGE. THEY ARE WATCHING US. THE TENTH LEVEL. THOUSANDS OF BATTLE DROIDS...
I UNDERSTAND. HAVE YOUR PEOPLE SEEK SHELTER. IF YOU HAVE WARRIORS, NOW IS THE TIME.
GENERAL KENOBI REPORTS THAT HE HAS LOCATED GENERAL GRIEVOUS ON UTAPAU. WE'RE PREPARING TO ATTACK.
THANK YOU, COMMANDER.
ANAKIN, I HAVE A VERY IMPORTANT ASSIGNMENT FOR YOU.
MASTER?

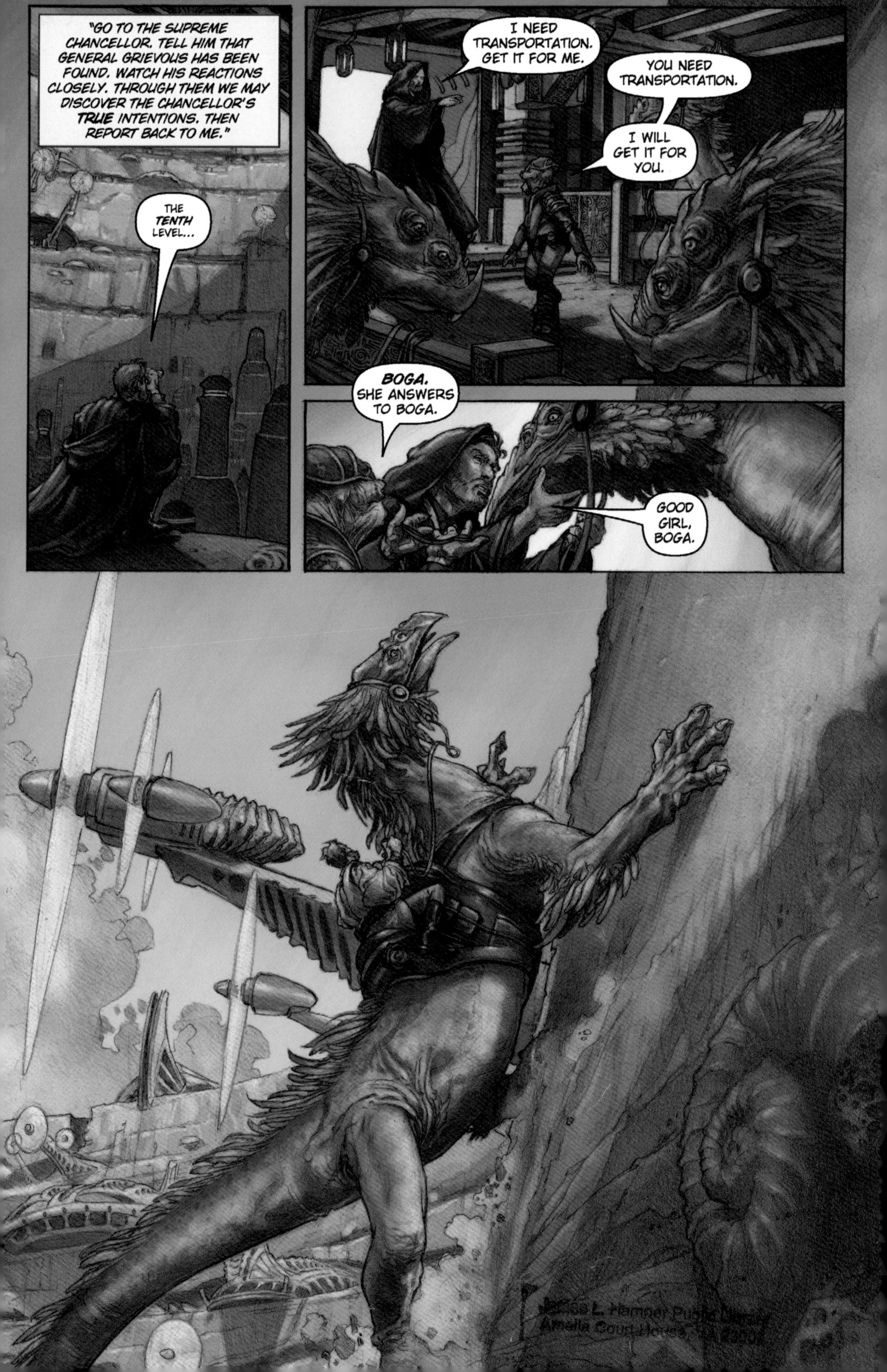
"GO TO THE SUPREME CHANCELLOR. TELL HIM THAT GENERAL GRIEVOUS HAS BEEN FOUND. WATCH HIS REACTIONS CLOSELY. THROUGH THEM WE MAY DISCOVER THE CHANCELLOR'S **TRUE** INTENTIONS. THEN REPORT BACK TO ME."
THE ***TENTH*** LEVEL...
I NEED TRANSPORTATION. GET IT FOR ME.
YOU NEED TRANSPORTATION.
I WILL GET IT FOR YOU.
BOGA. SHE ANSWERS TO BOGA.
GOOD GIRL, BOGA.

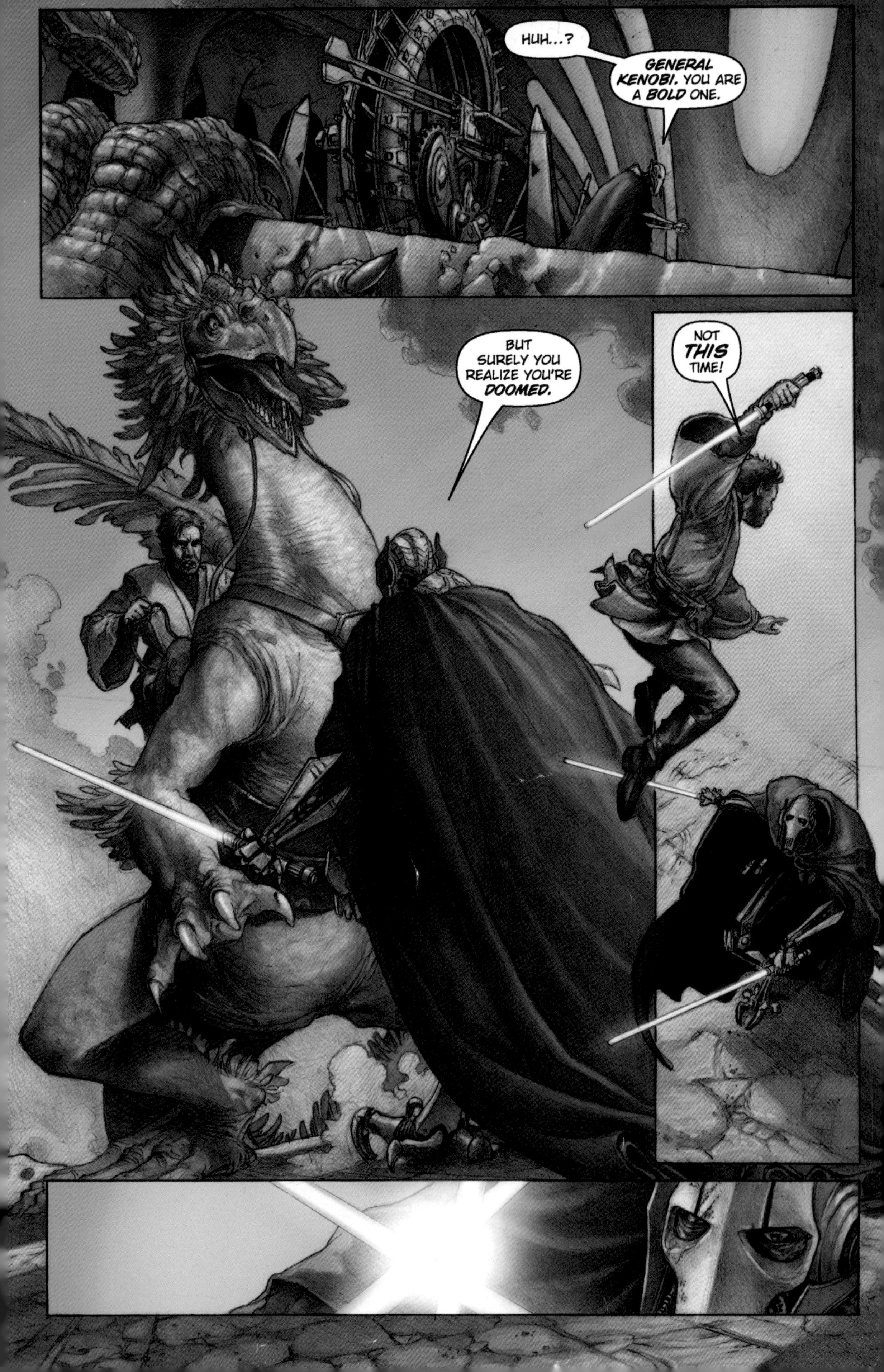
HUH...?
GENERAL KENOBI. YOU ARE A BOLD ONE.
BUT SURELY YOU REALIZE YOU'RE DOOMED.
NOT THIS TIME!

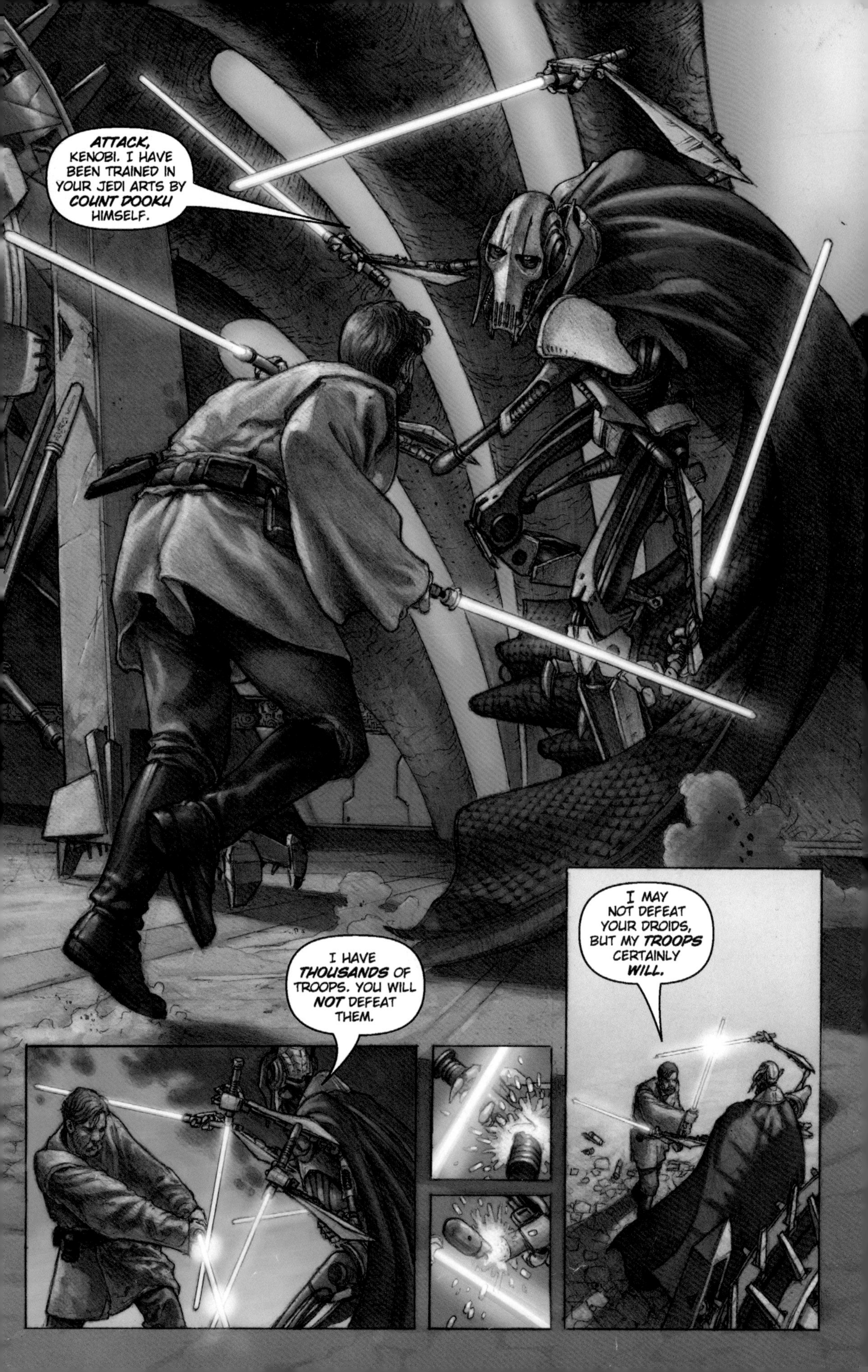
ATTACK, KENOBI. I HAVE BEEN TRAINED IN YOUR JEDI ARTS BY COUNT DOOKU HIMSELF.
I HAVE THOUSANDS OF TROOPS. YOU WILL NOT DEFEAT THEM.
I MAY NOT DEFEAT YOUR DROIDS, BUT MY TROOPS CERTAINLY WILL.

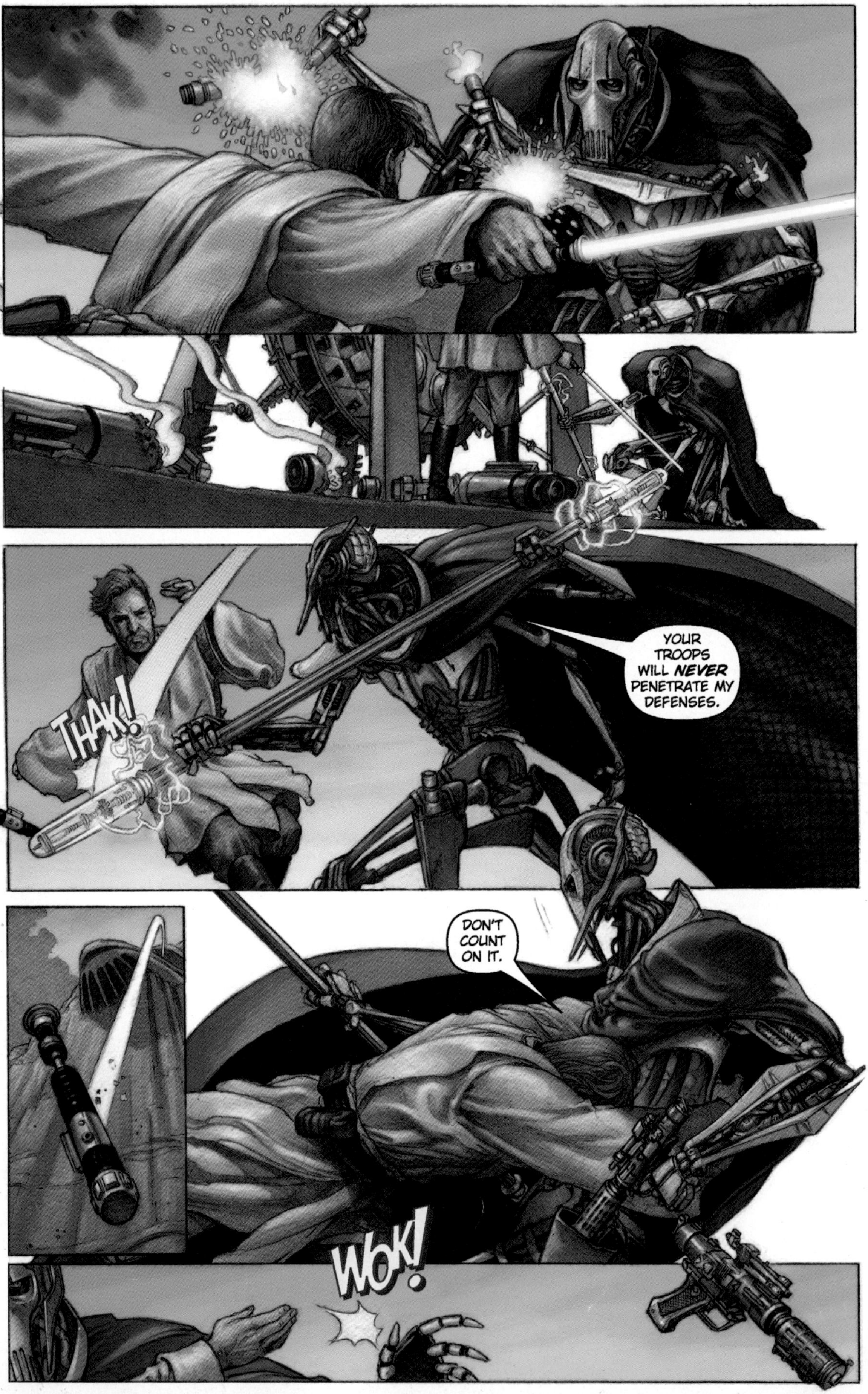
YOUR TROOPS WILL NEVER PENETRATE MY DEFENSES.
THAK!
DON'T COUNT ON IT.
WOK!

NNGH!

OOF!

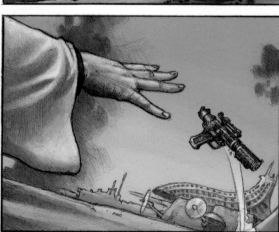

BOOW!
BOOW!
BOOW!

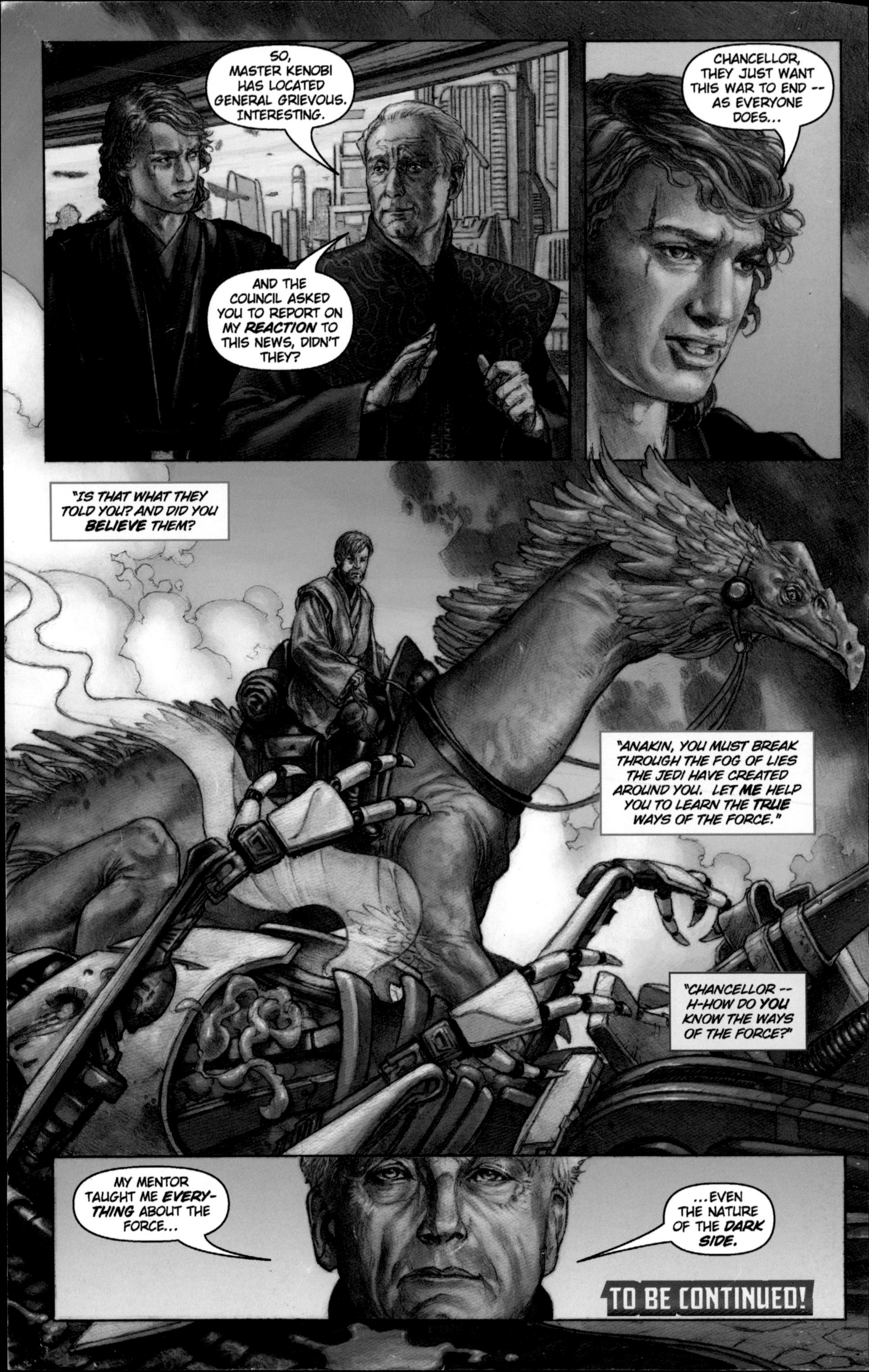
SO, MASTER KENOBI HAS LOCATED GENERAL GRIEVOUS. INTERESTING.
AND THE COUNCIL ASKED YOU TO REPORT ON MY **REACTION** TO THIS NEWS, DIDN'T THEY?
CHANCELLOR, THEY JUST WANT THIS WAR TO END -- AS EVERYONE DOES...
"IS THAT WHAT THEY TOLD YOU? AND DID YOU **BELIEVE** THEM?
"ANAKIN, YOU MUST BREAK THROUGH THE FOG OF LIES THE JEDI HAVE CREATED AROUND YOU. LET **ME** HELP YOU TO LEARN THE **TRUE** WAYS OF THE FORCE."
"CHANCELLOR -- H-HOW DO **YOU** KNOW THE WAYS OF THE FORCE?"
MY MENTOR TAUGHT ME **EVERYTHING** ABOUT THE FORCE...
...EVEN THE NATURE OF THE **DARK SIDE.**
TO BE CONTINUED!